D0373521

Can I Play Too?

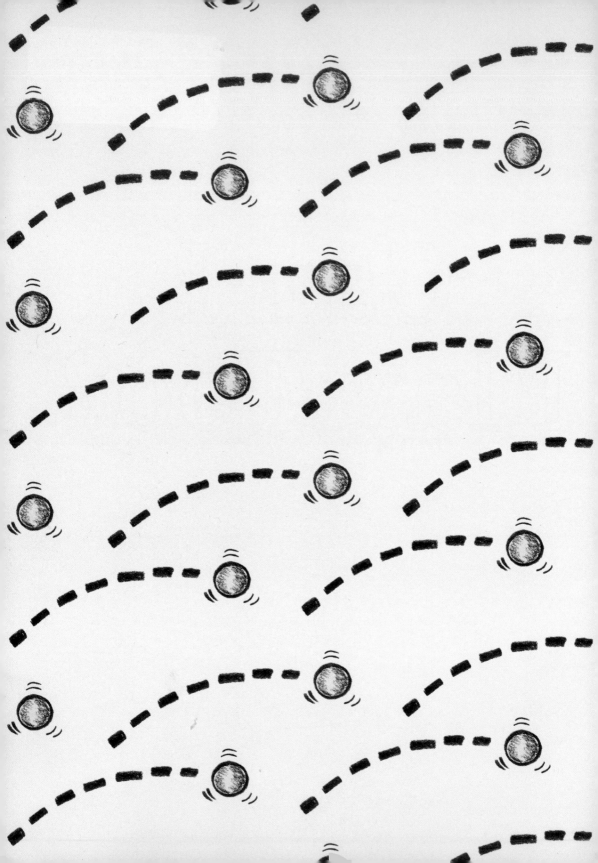

To Zat and Nellie
for playing along

No part of this publication may be reproduced, stored in a retrieval
system, or transmitted in any form or by any means, electronic, mechanical,
photocopying, recording, or otherwise, without written permission of the
publisher. For information regarding permission, write to
Hyperion Books for Children, an imprint of Disney Book Group,
125 West End Avenue, New York, NY 10023.

ISBN 978-0-545-84343-0

Text and illustrations copyright © 2010 by Mo Willems. All rights reserved.
Published by Scholastic Inc., 557 Broadway, New York, NY 10012,
by arrangement with Hyperion Books for Children, an imprint of
Disney Book Group. SCHOLASTIC and associated logos are trademarks
and/or registered trademarks of Scholastic Inc.

12 11   16 17 18 19 20/0

Printed in the U.S.A.   40

First Scholastic printing, February 2015

Can I Play Too?

By **Mo Willems**

An **ELEPHANT & PIGGIE** Book

SCHOLASTIC INC.

Piggie!

Let's play catch!

I will throw.

I will catch!

Can I play too?

11

12

13

17

19

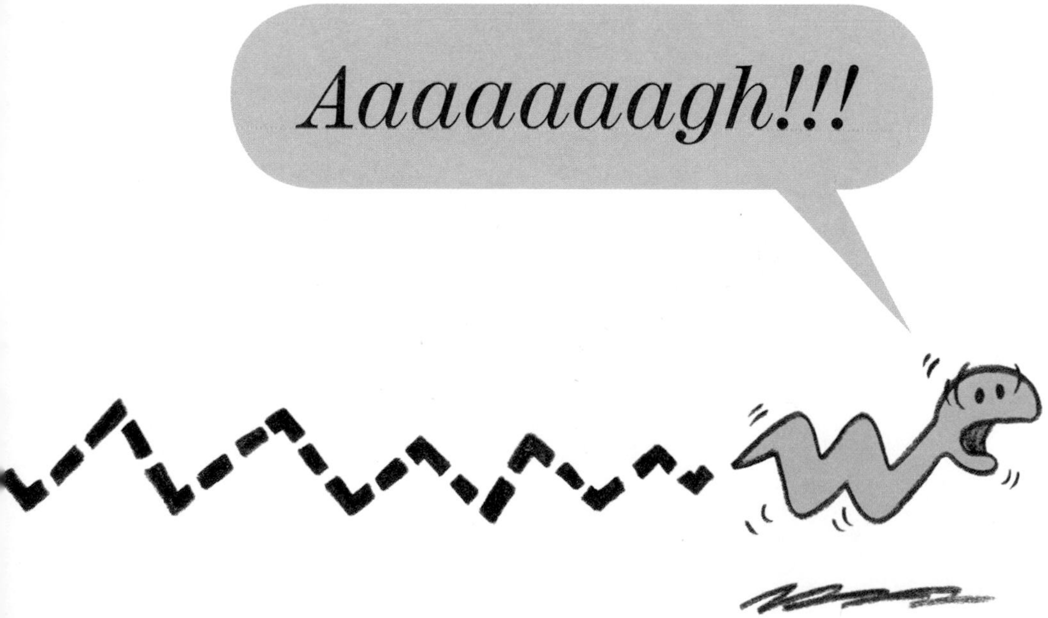
Aaaaaaaagh!!!

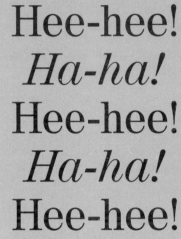

Hee-hee!
Ha-ha!
Hee-hee!
Ha-ha!
Hee-hee!

23

27

29

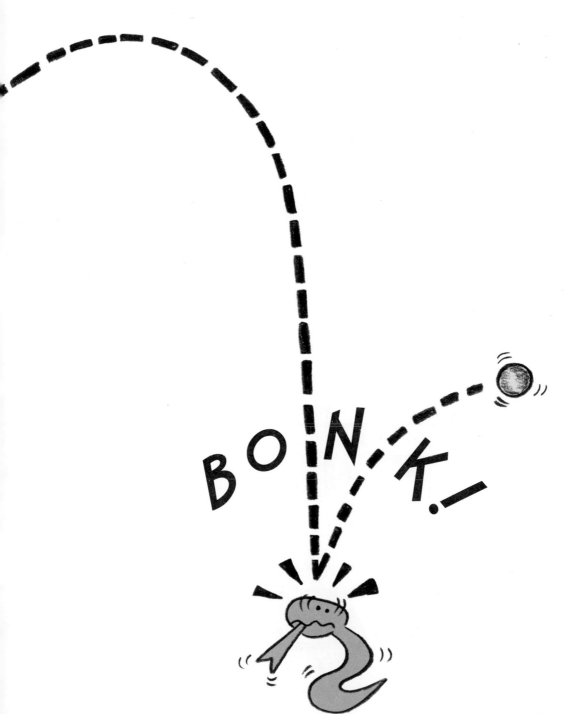

BONK!

31

33

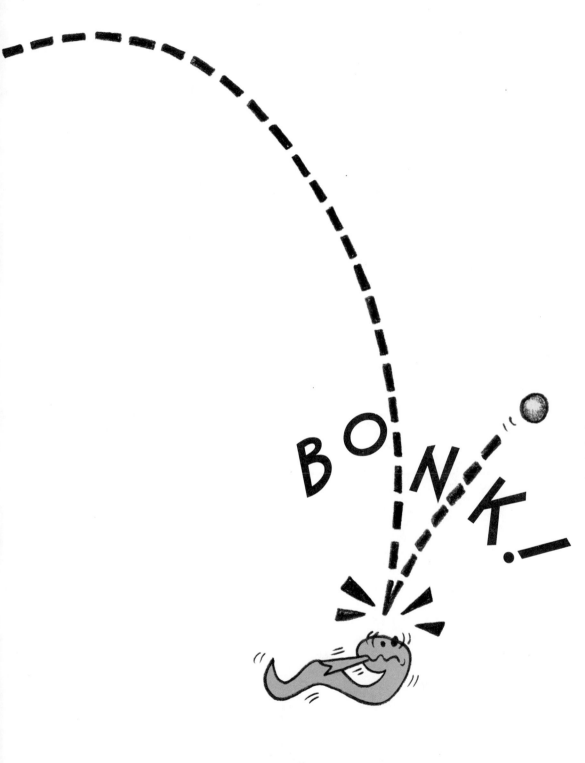

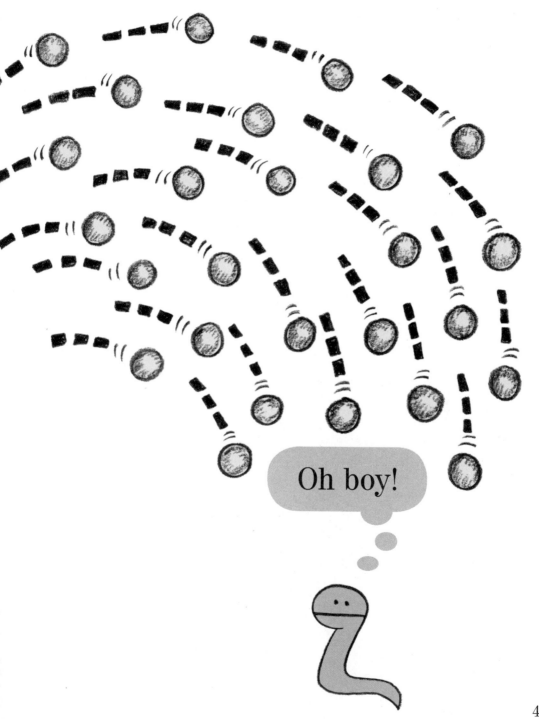

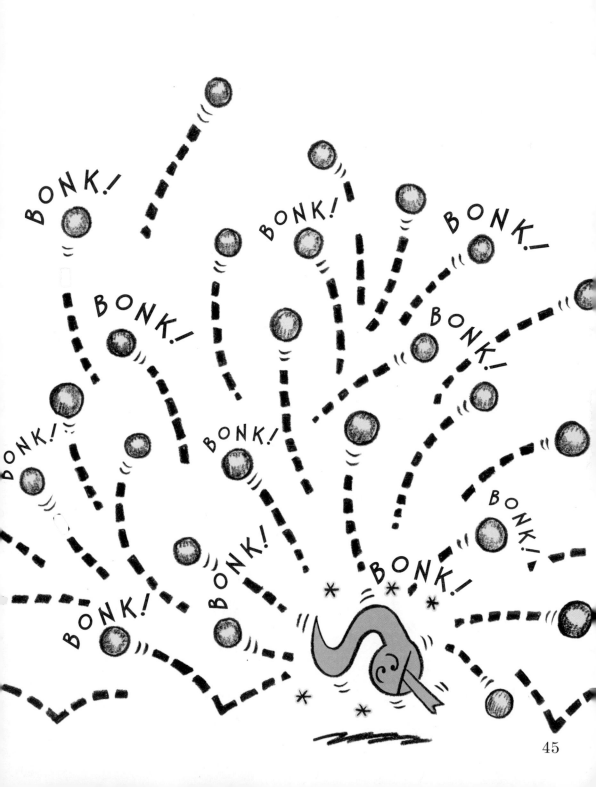

45

51

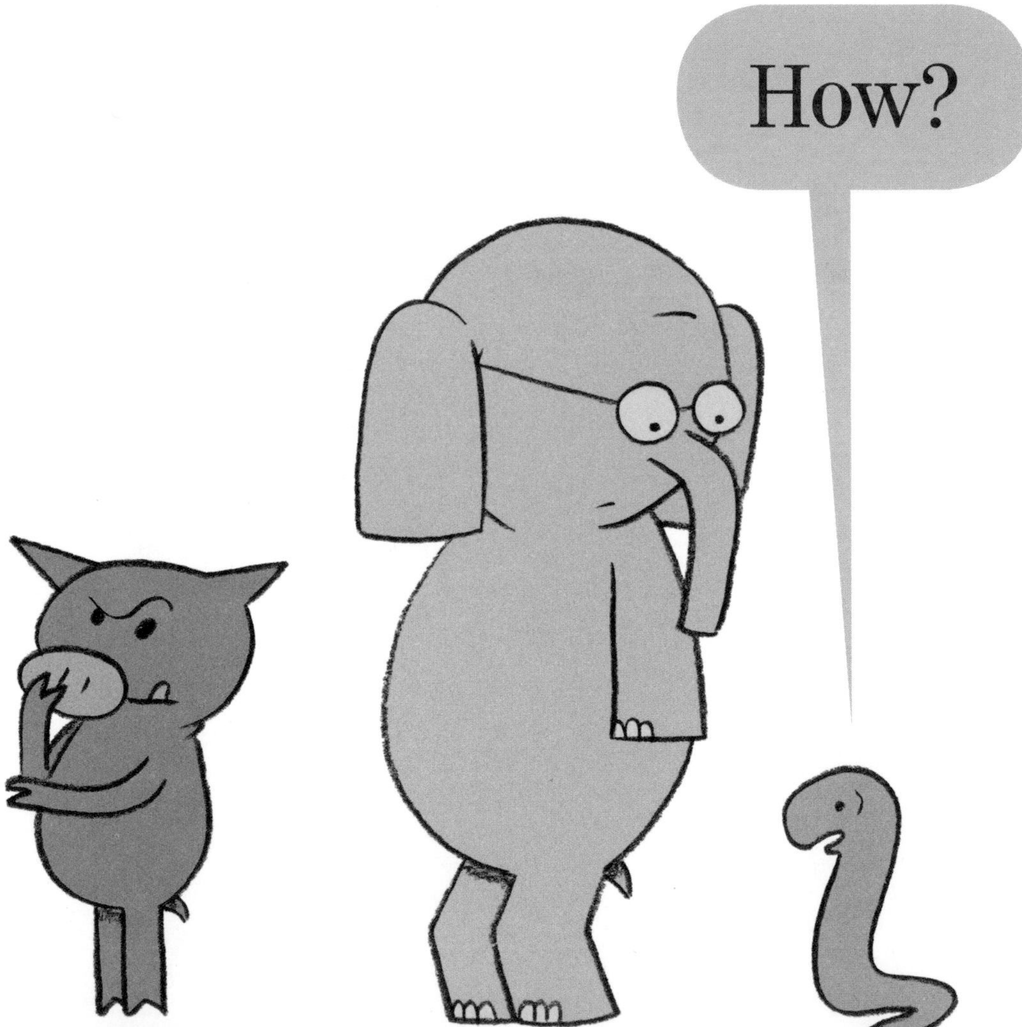
How?

Elephant and Piggie have more funny adventures in:

Today I Will Fly!

My Friend Is Sad

I Am Invited to a Party!

There Is a Bird on Your Head!

I Love My New Toy!

I Will Surprise My Friend!

Are You Ready to Play Outside?

Watch Me Throw the Ball!

Elephants Cannot Dance!

Pigs Make Me Sneeze!

I Am Going!